THE
CATNAPPING

Based on a True Story

Leslie Lampe Long

Illustrations by Jill O'Rourke

AuthorHouse™ LLC
1663 Liberty Drive
Bloomington, IN 47403
www.authorhouse.com
Phone: 1-800-839-8640

Jill O'Rourke (illustrations)

Published by AuthorHouse 03/18/2014

ISBN: 978-1-4918-6874-4 (sc)
ISBN: 978-1-4918-6878-2 (e)

Library of Congress Control Number: 2014904348

authorHOUSE®

Dedication

to my Granddaughter Ella, who knew from the start that
Sammy was a hero, and my husband, Bruce, who inspired me
never to give up hope

Acknowledgements

With much appreciation:
to the young book reviewers: Jackie Salwa and Morgan Busch
for the encouragement of the many supporters of this project: Ali Salwa,
Bobbi Warren, Deb Re, Karen Busch, Kate Cook, Margo Waite, Vin Albee
for the dedication of Detective Tom Jaquard (Officer Fuzz) of the Providence
Police, Nick's Taxi (Big Cat), Maureen Lockwood (Miss Kitty), to the
Pawtucket Police and to all ASPCA Shelters (Persnickitty Cat Rescue).

Chapter One

Sammy gives his sister, Jazzy, a wave of his paw to let her know he'll be right back. It's a freezing Saturday morning in January, so she'll stay in the Catillac while he goes to the flea market to get them some fresh mouse livers. Jazzy is soon asleep and dreaming of chasing mice.

Jazzy is in a deep, peaceful slumber when she hears a loud crash—the sound of broken glass. One of the Catillac windows shatters all around Jazzy as she leaps under the backseat.

What is going on? This isn't Sammy bounding through the window, but a big, scary burglar. *What is he doing in their Catillac?*

The burglar slinks down into Sammy's seat behind the wheel and starts the engine.

With a shopping cart full of mouse livers, Sammy exits the flea market, walks into the shopping center parking lot and locks his gaze onto a burglar sitting in the driver's seat of his Catillac. He abandons his shopping cart and runs after the car, yelling, "Stop that car! You've got Jazzy! You've got my sister!"

From under the backseat of the Catillac, the sounds of Sammy fade quickly. Jazzy can hear the wheels of the car screech as the burglar steps on the gas and speeds out of the parking lot. Jazzy is sure this is the last time she will see her brother.

Sammy's shouts are useless on this cold, rainy day. He runs as far as he can in the freezing rain as the Catillac speeds away.

"He's got Jazzy. Help me! Is there someone who can help?" He runs back to the flea market to find the manager. Together, they call the police.
"We're reporting a stolen Catillac and a catnapping. It's a dire emergency. Please come quickly." Minutes go by before the police arrive.

Jazzy can see wires hanging down where Sammy's keys used to be. As the car screeches and careens along, she hears the burglar calling someone.

"I'm comin' in with a Catillac. Nabbed it at the flea market." She hears the voice on the other end say, "Get your butt over here to the chop shop. You know the cops will be lookin' for that Catillac by now."
Jazzy trembles. She wants to escape from the car, but they are far away from the flea market, and she surely would never find her way back. *What is a chop shop?* she thinks, worried. *It sounds like a scary place where bad things happen. I just hope that they don't chop me up.*

After calling the police for help, Sammy fears the worst.

Does Jazzy know how much danger she's in? How will she protect herself? What will the burglar do when he finds Jazzy in the Catillac? Will he throw her out in the cold? Will he hurt her?

Jazzy stays quiet under the seat as the car turns into the parking lot of an old, giant building that sits on a hillside beside a river.

Jazzy sees the burglar move his eyes nervously around. "I just gotta get in and out of the chop shop. They get this Catillac unloaded and ready to chop up, then my partner gives me a ride home and mission accomplished."

As the burglar pulls up to the garage, Jazzy hears him yell "Okay, just open the door and let me in before anyone sees me."

"Whew," Jazzy says, exhaling quietly, "at least they're not going to chop me up." As the garage door opens, Jazzy hears sounds of drills, saws, and sparks flying. Choppers are chopping up Catillacs just like theirs. A door beside the garage opens, and one of the choppers leans out.

"Bad news, Bud. There's no room for your Catillac in the chop shop right now. We're full with cars to chop," he yells.

"Well, what do you expect me to do?" Bud yells back.

"Just unload the stuff inside and bring the car back tomorrow." Bud, the burglar, jumps out and, with some of the choppers, starts pulling stuff out of the back of the Catillac—mostly litter bags and Catty Shack souvenirs. Jazzy feels a blast of cold air.

Then, all of a sudden, a big, dirty hand grabs her by her trembling tail. A gruff voice blares, "What's this? Your little pet, Bud? Oh, how sweet."

"Let's throw him in the river. We have enough to worry about," another says.

"Nah, I'll take him into the warehouse and let him out somewhere inside," Bud says.

With that, Bud drops Jazzy in a box beside the door. The cover of the box slams shut.

"Bud, get that cat outta here," one of the choppers says. Jazzy feels herself being carried up some stairs and hears Bud say, "This tin roof over the shop is a good place to leave her." She feels warm metal under her box.

From cracks in the side of the box, she sees that she is on a small tin roof overlooking the chop shop. The noise is deafening—screeching, buzzing, and crunching. There are cars, mostly Catillacs, just like hers. She sees the choppers saw through the metal roof of a car, cutting the top in half and worries,

The shop is chopping up cars, and our Catillac is coming back tomorrow to be chopped up like all the others.

Then she hears Bud say, "This car's clean. I'll bring it back tomorrow." He backs their Catillac away from the chop shop. It would not be the last time Jazzy hears Bud's voice.

When Officer Fuzz arrives at the flea market, Sammy gives him a description of his Catillac and tells the officer that his sister was in the car when it was stolen. Officer Fuzz offers little hope, "Chances are the car is headed straight for a chop shop. Those burglars chop those cars up and sell the parts as quick as they can. We'll put out an all-points bulletin and get looking right away. We'll call you a cab so you can get home."

A cab driver named Big Cat from the Big Cat Taxi Company arrives at the store to pick up Sammy and his cart of mouse livers. Sammy tells Big Cat the story of his stolen Catillac and the catnapping of Jazzy.

"Dude, that's some bad luck—some really bad luck." Big Cat is outraged. "You've gotta get on this right away. Get the word out. Call the TV stations; they'd love this story. Call the radio stations too. Gotta get moving on this before it's too late!" Big Cat's ideas got Sammy thinking. It would be a long shot, but he had to do something.

He would get the word out right away to anyone who might find his sister on a freezing January day.

Chapter two

Jazzy shakes with fear when one of the choppers approaches the box and says in a voice that his buddies can't hear, "It's getting pretty warm up here. I'll let you out before it gets too hot. Maybe you'll find a way to live." With that, he opens the lid to the box and says, "Now scram, cat."

Jazzy scurries out of the carrier to find a hiding place away from the chop shop. So far, she escaped being thrown out of the car onto a highway and being thrown into the freezing cold river. Now she has to figure out how to stay alive.

Jazzy runs for the door, but all the doors are shut. She cannot escape to the outside. It's dark in this part of the warehouse, and there are boxes everywhere. She finally spots a good hiding place behind a box that says "Patio Table" on the side. She scrunches herself up really small and hides between the box and the wall.

She wakes up the next day to the smell of food and tiptoes out from the hiding place toward the smells coming from behind a nearby door. She hears voices from behind the door of a small kitchen.

"Hey, Sal, want some coffee?" one of the voices says.

"Yeah. We got a furniture order we got to get out today, so I'll have a cup and head down to the loading dock."

"Okay, I'll go back and get the boxes ready," the other worker said.

Suddenly, the door opens. Inside, Jazzy sees milk and sandwiches. Her stomach rumbles with hunger. But she worries that the choppers might hurt her or throw her in the river. She's so close, but she just can't chance it. She runs away to find another hiding place. This time, she spots a tall box that is empty and open at the top. On the side, it says "Chaise Lounge." She thinks, *I'll hide here until I can run into the kitchen without being noticed.*

The worker getting the boxes must have heard Jazzy when she jumped into the tall box.

"What's that noise? Hey, Sal, I think there's something back here. It's larger than a mouse for sure."

Jazzy hears him walking from box to box, opening and closing the tops. Her heart is pounding.

"It is must be in here somewhere," the worker says to Sal.

"Never mind that. We got to get this order moving. Let's check out the loading dock," Sal replies.

The door to the kitchen has been open all this time, and Jazzy still smells milk and sandwiches. She listens from inside the tall box as the workers walk over to a window to inspect the loading dock two stories below. She then hears Sal talking about the garage where she was yanked out of the Catillac yesterday.

"You know those cars that have been driving into the garage? I've been seeing those cars go in that garage and not come out. Most of them have been Catillacs."

"What do you suppose is going on in that garage?" the other worker asks. "You think that might be a chop shop operation in there?"

"Yeah," Sal says, "and I'm not going anywhere near it if it is. I'll call the police and have them check it out. Let's make that call right now."

Jazzy hears Sal and the other worker walk back to their office. They walk past her box and into the kitchen. The door closes behind them, and with that go all the smells of food and milk.

Chapter Three

After Sammy's talk with Big Cat, the cabbie, he hopes that if he acts fast, he might be able to find Jazzy. Big Cat told Sammy about cats who had been lost and then found, usually after just a few days.

That night, Sammy creates a poster with a picture of Jazzy from Christmas. The poster reads, "Have you seen Jazzy? Gray Tabby. Lost when Catillac was stolen." He takes the posters to all the rescue shelters, fire stations, flea markets, and police stations in the area. He places an advertisement in all the local newspapers and offers a reward for the safe return of Jazzy.

Sammy figures that Jazzy cannot survive long in the freezing weather. He imagines Jazzy being thrown out onto a street in the cold. Each day that goes by is surely torture for poor Jazzy. Each day that goes by is unbearable for Sammy, but the very next day, Sammy receives a response from the newspaper ad.

HAVE YOU SEEN JAZZY?

Gray Tabby Cat lost January 22nd

When Catillac stolen. Could be anywhere in area.

REWARD

Meanwhile, back at the warehouse, Jazzy awakes with a jolt to the sound of police sirens outside. She sees the whirling red lights flashing on the ceiling above her box. Something big must be happening.

The whole building shakes when the police pound on the garage door, shouting to the choppers, "Open up! Police!"

One of the policemen shows his badge and yells, "Officer Fuzz in charge here." There is a great commotion inside the shop as Officer Fuzz and other policemen burst in. The choppers scramble to escape. Tools clank as they drop. Saws buzz out of control as they scrape along the floor.

Jazzy hears one of the choppers trying to run away. Officer Fuzz yells, "Oh no you don't, fella. Get back down here. You and all your chopper buddies are under arrest for the possession of stolen goods."

Jazzy hears the police grabbing the choppers in the chop shop and forcing them, one by one, into handcuffs, then putting them into waiting police cars. A little while later, the police return, and she hears a big locking sound. "This chop shop is officially out of business!" Officer Fuzz says as he slams the garage door and locks it shut.

The sounds get more muffled, and before long, there are hardly any sounds coming from the chop shop garage.

Meanwhile, back at the search for Jazzy, it's the very first day of his newspaper ad when the phone rings.

Sammy hears the magic words.

"We've found your gray tabby," the voice on the phone declares. The caller sounds like he is in a hurry, but he also sounds certain that he has found Jazzy.

"You have Jazzy? Great!" Sammy is overjoyed that the newspaper ad worked. "Where can I pick her up?" Sammy asks the caller as his heart leaps with joy.

"Not so fast, dude. You said there's a reward. I wanna know what the reward is," the caller demands. Sammy starts to wonder about this caller, but he also wants his sister back. He tells him the reward is two hundred dollars.

"Two? How about three hundred?" the caller says. It is impossible to put a price on how much Sammy wants Jazzy back, so he says "Okay, three hundred dollars."

It is clear the caller has some kind of a plan when he says, "Okay, you send me the money, and I'll hold on to your Jazzy until I get the cash. Once I've got it, I'll tell you where you can pick her up."

Sammy now knows that this is a trick. "Do you think I'm stupid? You don't have my sister!" Sammy screams angrily as he hears the phone on the other end click off.

27

Sammy has a sick feeling in his stomach because he was tricked. *I want to report this to Officer Fuzz,* Sammy thinks as he calls the number back to see if he can figure out who the caller was. Someone picks up the phone. It doesn't sound like the same voice.

"Are you the caller who claimed to have my sister?" Sammy demands.

"Look, fella, this is a prison pay phone. You got the wrong number!"

With that, Sammy hangs up the phone. Jazzy is in danger of losing her life, if she is even still alive, and Sammy is being tricked by crooks. It has been three very cold days, and it is even less likely Jazzy is still alive.

Sammy has gotten the word out about the stolen car and his missing sister in newspapers and on posters. The word has spread, and Sammy starts to hear stories about when other cars were stolen.

There are stories of lost pets and cars and how they were found. One car was stolen with a Pekinese dog in it. The dog was found the day the car was located, six days after it was stolen. To Sammy, it sounds too good to be true, but it gives him hope. It has now been eight days since the catnapping.

Maybe tomorrow, Sammy hopes.

Hiding inside her box, Jazzy knows she is completely alone now— no chop shop sounds and no food smells. She is alone in a big warehouse and hiding in a tall box. It has been more than eight days since she has had food or water. It is quiet now and safer to leave the tall box.

But when she jumps to get out of the box, she falls back against the side. Her legs are weak from being so hungry. She keeps trying to jump out of the box, but each time, she falls back, dizzy and exhausted. She keeps scraping her legs on the cardboard edge, and pretty soon, her legs and paws are raw and bleeding. She falls back into the box, feeling hungry, helpless, and alone.

The warehouse is completely dark, and all she hears now is the howling of the wind outside and the creaking of the walls as the bitter cold air seeps in. She cries big cat tears and thinks, *I know I'll never see Sammy again.*

It has now been ten days since Jazzy was catnapped, when Sammy receives a call from a Miss Kitty. She says that she and her husband feed homeless cats every day at sunset, and a new cat matching Jazzy's description appeared with the other cats a few days ago.

"Why don't you come join us while we feed the cats today?" asks Miss Kitty. Sammy agrees.

Big Cat drives Sammy to the house where Miss Kitty lives, high on a hill overlooking the bay. Miss Kitty quickly says, "Come on in. I'm preparing food for the cats now." When Sammy walks into Miss Kitty's kitchen, he's amazed to see her scooping cat food from giant cans. Sammy wonders how many cats they could possibly be feeding.

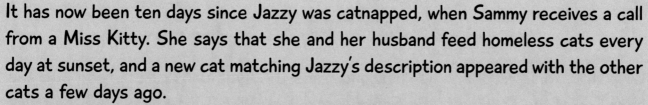

With that, Miss Kitty and her husband place the huge pans of cat food into the open bed of their pickup truck. Sammy gets in with Big Cat to follow. As the truck moves slowly down the hill toward the bay, cats appear from everywhere—cats to the right and cats to the left. There are so many cats surrounding them that it is difficult to drive behind the truck.

The truck finally stops by an abandoned house at the water's edge. It is overgrown with weeds, and shingles are falling off. There are also broken windows, and paint is peeling. As Miss Kitty unloads each pan of cat food, cats swarm to eat it. Cats are in the large yard as far as eye can see. Perhaps there are more than 100 cats, and Miss Kitty points in the direction of the water's edge.

"There's the cat I told you about. This one appeared a few days after you lost your sister."

Sammy strains to pick one cat out of the swarm. "That shy one over there," Miss Kitty continues. Jazzy was a shy cat, so Sammy waits to see the small tabby get closer. But when he gets a good look, Sammy sees clearly that this is not Jazzy. Disappointed and exasperated, Sammy gets closer to the small tabby cat.

Sammy wants more than anything to get through this nightmare. Maybe he could just will away the pain of losing Jazzy. *This cat is so like Jazzy, looks like Jazzy, acts like Jazzy ... maybe I could just take her home instead.* He feels so guilty even thinking it, and he quickly comes to his senses.

Sammy thinks for a moment about what went through his mind. It meant that he had given up hope. Here he was, ten days of searching and following leads about his missing Jazzy.

In a resolute voice, he says to himself, "Hope. Hope is all you have left, Sammy. How can you give up hope that you will find Jazzy?"

Sammy feels ashamed that he would give up on finding Jazzy. He thanks the cat herders. Their caring for homeless cats was something Sammy would remember every time he looked up at their house, high on the hill overlooking the bay.

Mrs. Persnickitty Cat Rescue

From my paw to yours

Persnickitty1@catmail.com

Sammy is determined to be hopeful when, two days later, he gets yet another call from a concerned cat lover. This call is from Persnickitty Cat Rescue.

But Sammy is at work in his office at the Caterpillar Company—forty-five minutes away. Determined, but also afraid of being disappointed again, he says, "You know I've made a couple of long trips to locate Jazzy only to be disappointed. I'd like to ask you a favor," Sammy says. "Do you think you could put Jazzy on the phone with me?"

"The cat's here with the phone by her ear. Go ahead," says Mrs. Persnickitty.

"Hi, Jazzy," Sammy says. "I miss you." Before Jazzy could even answer, Mrs. Persnickitty grabs the phone and sounds excited.

"She recognizes your voice!"

"That's my sister, Jazzy," Sammy says.

"Yes, no doubt about it," Mrs. Persnickitty says.

Sammy bounces up from his chair, speeds out of his office, and heads right to Persnickitty Cat Rescue. He is filled with anticipation and hope. When he gets to the shelter, Mrs. Persnickitty brings out the cat that Sammy talked to on the phone. Alas, this is not Jazzy. Sammy is appreciative but more discouraged than ever.

That night, alone, weak, and trapped in a box, Jazzy dreams she is a bird. Wings grow where her paws were—big strong wings that lift her right up and out of the box.

She dreams of food piled high on a plate for her in the kitchen and milk in a dish fit only for a queen. In her dream, she is a queen. She has a crown and Sammy and everyone in the kitchen are happy to see her lapping up the milk. She awakes from her dream to the sound of police sirens.

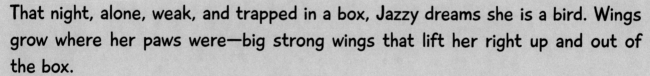

Chapter four

On the
fourteenth
day, Sammy receives
another phone call. This call is from
Officer Fuzz, who tells Sammy that the
police found his stolen Catillac.

"We apprehended a known burglar while he was
driving a Catillac with a broken front window. We
have the car and the burglar in custody. We need you
to come down to the station to identify him."
Thinking of all the stories he had heard about stolen cars,
Sammy exclaims, "That's incredible! Was Jazzy in the car?"
Officer Fuzz says, "No Jazzy, but we have your Catillac." Sammy replies excitedly,
"Thank you, I'll be right down to the station!"

When Sammy arrives at the station, the police ask him to identify the suspect from a lineup. Looking at the lineup, Sammy remembers the burglar in his Catillac from two weeks before.

Once Sammy identifies the burglar, he asks Officer Fuzz to find out where the burglar left Jazzy. When he returns, Officer Fuzz says to Sammy, "He left Jazzy somewhere inside the warehouse where the chop shop had been before it was shut down. We'll take the burglar there right away while you go to claim your Catillac."

Jazzy awakes from her dream to the sound of police sirens, voices talking, and feet clanging up the stairs not far from her box. She hears a familiar voice say, "I let the cat out here on this tin roof."

That is Bud, the burglar who broke into our car, she thinks.

She then hears Sal say, "And, Officer Fuzz, this is right beside my furniture warehouse."

"So let's see if we can find her," Officer Fuzz says.

She hears Officer Fuzz, Burglar Bud, and Sal lifting boxes, walking around the warehouse.

No way, she thought, *I'd rather die here than risk being hurt.* She is still and quiet in her box.

Then she hears Officer Fuzz say, "Well, I have to return to the station. I'll let her brother know where the burglar left her."

Her brother? Jazzy wondered if Officer Fuzz was talking about Sammy.

"We found where the burglar left Jazzy," Officer Fuzz told Sammy. "A warehouse over by the river where a chop shop had been. We looked for your sister but didn't have any luck. You can go over and look for her yourself. The super will be there to let you in. His office is around the back of the building behind the boiler."

Sammy is achingly hopeful. It's been fifteen days since Jazzy disappeared, and Sammy is heading over to the warehouse where she was last seen.

When Sammy gets to the warehouse, he is taken aback. "How will I ever find Jazzy in this huge building?" He is overwhelmed but hopeful.

It snowed the day before, and no one is around on Sunday. It is eerie. He is completely alone, and this is the building where crooks chopped up stolen cars and who knows what else.

Just then, he hears a loud engine that sounds like it is coming into the dark alley. Sammy is trapped in the alley with no escape. He quickly hides behind a dumpster so no one can see him. He waits, listening and trembling at the sound of the engine that keeps coming closer and closer.

The loud engine noise is coming from a snowplow clearing parking spaces.

Sammy calls, "Hey, are you the super?"

"No, sir, I own the lawn furniture factory over that garage," the snow plower says as he points across the parking lot.

Sammy explains, "Well, my Catillac was stolen. My sister was in the car at the time, and she could be somewhere in this building. I came here to put my posters around the building."

"Oh, you're her brother!" he exclaims. I'm the one who called in the sting on that chop shop right next to my business. Cars were coming into the garage and not coming out. My name is Sal. Officer Fuzz was here yesterday. I helped them look all over for your sister, but no luck. We did find where the burglar let your sister out. Would that be helpful?"

Sammy couldn't believe his ears. All this searching, and now he will find out exactly where Jazzy was last seen.

"Here's where they let her out," says Sal. "On this tin roof over where the chop shop was." Sammy looks at the small tin roof, and his heart aches. This may be where Jazzy was last alive. He tries not to give up hope.

As he scans the huge space of the warehouse from where they are standing, he asks, "Sal, if you were Jazzy, how far could you run inside the walls of this warehouse before you found a way outside?"

Sal points in a circle to the four walls around them. "You mean, there's no door to the outside?" Sammy asks. "No, we keep all the doors on this floor closed all the time, even the kitchen door, which we go in and out of a lot. It's almost always closed."

He asks Sal to hang back while he searches the area.

"Jazzy, hey, Jazzy," he calls. "It's your brother Sammy." He walks softly around the expanse of boxes. Silence. "Jazzy, hey, Jazzy." Again, nothing. After several tries, he walks back to where Sal is waiting and heaves a big discouraged sigh.

Jazzy tries to move her tail, but she can't. She can't move her paws. She can't move her legs. Her stomach is hollow, and she feels numb. Her mouth is so dry she can't even lick her dusty paws.

She drifts off to a strange kind of sleep where she doesn't feel anything, like she's floating. That's when she dreams that she sees Sammy coming into the warehouse. She can see that Sammy is lost and wandering around. She dreams that she calls to Sammy. He doesn't recognize Jazzy's call at first, so she calls again.

Then Sal remembers the noise in one of the boxes, "You know, Sammy, I just remembered that one of my workers heard a noise outside my kitchen the other day. He said it sounded larger than a mouse. We explored the boxes to find where the noise came from, but we had no luck."

Sammy's heart is pounding fast as he tiptoes over to the area outside the kitchen where Sal said he heard the noise. "Hey, Jazzy. It's Sammy." Nothing but quiet. Then he hears a barely audible squeaky sound, a sound Sammy doesn't recognize.

"Jazzy." Again, he hears the soft squeaky sound. "Jazzy?" Again, the sound. It's coming from a box with the words "Chaise Lounge" on the side. Sammy walks slowly over to the box and looks inside.

Huddled in the corner of the box is a small ball of dusty fur that is barely recognizable. "Jazzy?" Sammy, almost afraid, whispers, and the ball of dust responds again with the squeaky sound. Sammy may not recognize her, but this ball of dusty fur recognizes Sammy.

"Jazzy!" Sammy exclaims, as he carefully tips the box to lift the fragile fur ball out of the box.

Sammy and Jazzy have found each other.

"I have some milk in my kitchen," Sal says with tears in his eyes. Sammy holds Jazzy in his arms, wiping the dust from her face and ears as Sal opens the door and walks them into the kitchen.

Jazzy laps up the bowl of milk as Sammy and Sal look on in wonder. The dust on the top of Jazzy's head makes a ring like a golden brown crown. Sammy is overjoyed at the miracle. Still overwhelmed, he hugs Sal in thanks. It has been fifteen days. Jazzy barely weighs three pounds now and was as close to death as a cat could be. Even one more day might have been the end for her.

Just then, Officer Fuzz knocks on Sal's door and comes into the kitchen to see Sammy and a ball of fur that must be his sister, Jazzy. Here she is, alive and drinking milk.

Sammy, holding Jazzy's paw, says, "It's a miracle! Sal, can you get Big Cat, Miss Kitty and Mrs. Persnickitty?"

"Miracles do happen. We got the burglar, and you got your Catillac back," says Officer Fuzz.

After hearing the news, Big Cat says to Sammy, "And miracle of miracles, you and your sister found each other!"

Jazzy replies, "Prayers really can come true if you just don't give up hope."

In the parking lot, Sammy holds Jazzy as they thank Sal, Officer Fuzz, Miss Kitty, Mrs. Persnikitty and Big Cat in his taxi.

They say, "Thank you, all of you, for without you, we might have given up hope!" Sammy and Jazzy get into their Catillac—the first time they both had been in the car in fifteen days—and wave good-bye as they pass the huge factory warehouse on the hill by the river.

epilogue

It was a miracle that Sal had been there plowing snow and that he had been there with the police the day before. It was a miracle that Sal called in the sting on the chop shop. It was a miracle that the Providence Police found the car and the carrier and that Jazzy and Sammy never gave up hope.

---

112 - The Happy Column

CAR FOUND - CAT FOUND:
Miracles Do Happen. Gray Tabby cat found after missing Jeep Cherokee located. Thanks to the Providence Police, Sal, and all Cat Lovers Who Cared Enough To Help.

It was a miracle that Jazzy went on to live another nine years.

HAVE YOU SEEN JAZZY?

Gray Tabby Cat lost January 22nd

when Jeep Cherokee was stolen
May be found in round cloth carrier which
looks like a suitcase.
Could be anywhere in area.

REWARD

About the Author: Leslie Lampe Long is a cat lover, psychoanalyst and career coach living in Providence, Rhode Island. This is Leslie's second children's book project, the first, "Do Not Be Sad," is a collection of children's art and letters sent to the FDNY after the tragedy of September 11.

About the Illustrator: Jill O'Rourke has a Bachelors of Fine Arts in Illustration from the Art Institute of Boston at Lesley University. Jill creates custom illustrations for both residential and commercial clients.

Printed in the United States
By Bookmasters